This book belongs to

Katie

" Merry Christmas! "

Love, Denise

Young Readers Book Club presents...

Warm in Winter

Erica Silverman

Illustrated by Michael J. Deraney

Macmillan Publishing Company   New York
Collier Macmillan Publishers   London

To Linda Torn, Sue Alexander,
Ann Paul, Karen Winnick,
and Jane Alexander Stewart,
with thanks
—E.S.

For Jodi, Scott, Kellee,
Andrea, and Holli
—M.J.D.

Macmillan Publishing Company, 866 Third Avenue, New York, NY 10022. Collier Macmillan Canada, Inc.

B   C   D   1 2 3
The text of this book is set in 16 point Goudy Old Style.
The illustrations are rendered in pencil and watercolor.
Library of Congress Cataloging-in-Publication Data • Silverman, Erica.
Warm in winter/Erica Silverman; illustrated by Michael J. Deraney.—1st American ed.   p.   cm.
Summary: A cozy visit with her friend Rabbit, featuring a soft flannel nightie and hot carrot soup,
convinces a skeptical Badger that you really can be warm in winter.
ISBN 0-02-782661-9
[1. Badgers—Fiction. 2. Rabbits—Fiction. 3. Winter—Fiction. 4. Friendship—Fiction.]
I. Deraney, Michael J., ill. II. Title. PZ7.S58625War 1989   [E]—dc 19   88-22691 CIP   AC

Badger and her new friend, Rabbit, played hide-and-seek in the meadow. At lunchtime they sat side by side at the lake. They munched on crunchy carrots. They drank ice-cold lemonade.

Badger jumped her black checker over Rabbit's red one.

"Ah," said Badger. "What could be better than a good game of checkers?" She raised her snout to the sky. "And what could be warmer than a sunny summer's day?"

"Winter," said Rabbit. "I like it better when it's warm in winter."

"Ha!" Badger laughed. "How can it ever be warm in winter?"

"Wait and see," said Rabbit.

Summer came to an end. Badger and Rabbit
took long walks every day.

They played in piles of autumn leaves.

One night the icy fingers of the winter wind tapped on Badger's window. In the morning the air was thick with snow.

Badger found a letter by her door. It said,

> Dear Badger,
> Hurry over and you will see
> how warm in winter we can be.
> > Your friend,
> > Rabbit

"Warm?" Badger peeked outside. The cold nipped at her nose. Quickly she closed the door.

Badger set up the checkerboard. She moved a black checker up one square. Then she stared at the red checkers. "It's no fun playing checkers alone," she muttered.

She got out her crayons and started to draw.
"Rabbit would like my picture."

She looked at Rabbit's invitation. She looked
out the window at the falling snow. Badger sighed.

Then she put on a sweater, a vest, two pairs of
socks, boots, a hat, a scarf, two pairs of mittens,
a jacket, and a heavy coat.

She picked up her picture and stepped outside.
"Brrrr." Badger shivered.

Crunch, crunch, crunch. Snow filled her boots.
"My paws feel like lumps of ice!"

Badger huffed as she tromped up the hill. Her
hat blew off. "The wind is biting my ears!"

"My picture!" She watched it fly away.
Snow blew in her eyes. "Now I can't see
where I'm going."

Plop! A clump of snow fell on her head. "How
can it ever be warm in winter?" grumbled Badger.

She started to run. "Help!" Down she slid.
Splunk! She landed in a snowbank.

"I'll never be warm again." Badger cried.
Tears froze on her snout.

At last Badger arrived at Rabbit's door.
"O-o-open up," she called. "I'm cold and wet,
and the wind blew my picture away."

"Poor Badger," said Rabbit. She helped Badger out of her wet clothes. She gave her a flannel nightie, fuzzy slippers, a floppy nightcap, and a soft robe.

"Stand by the fire," said Rabbit. She disappeared into the kitchen.

Rabbit returned with mugs of carrot soup and chunks of clover bread dripping with honey.

"Mmmmmmm." Steam from the soup curled around Badger's snout.

Badger and Rabbit sat on the floor with
crayons and paper. Pinecones crackled in the
fireplace. Flickering shadows danced on the walls.
"I like your picture," said Rabbit.

"Here," said Badger. "It's for you."

"And I made this one for you." Rabbit gave
Badger her picture. "Now let's play checkers,"
she said.

Badger watched Rabbit set up the checkerboard.
She took a sip of the soup Rabbit had made
for her. She snuggled deep in the nightie Rabbit
had given her. She looked at the picture Rabbit
had drawn for her. Then she looked out the
window at the falling snow.

"You know, Rabbit," said Badger, "being here with you makes me feel..." Badger stopped. She stared at her friend.

"Feel what?" said Rabbit.

Badger smiled. "Warm," she said. "Warm in winter."

Then she picked up a black checker and started to play.